The Pet Keeper Fairies

For Evie Tolley, a wonderful
fairy god-daughter

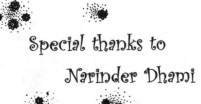

Special thanks to
Narinder Dhami

ORCHARD BOOKS
338 Euston Road, London NW1 3BH
Orchard Books Australia
Hachette Children's Books
Level 17/207 Kent Street, Sydney, NSW 2000
A Paperback Original

First published in Great Britain in 2006
Rainbow Magic is a registered trademark of Working Partners Limited.
Series created by Working Partners Limited, London W6 OQT

ISBN 978 1 84616 170 4
9 10 8

Printed in Great Britain

Bella
the Bunny
Fairy

by Daisy Meadows

illustrated by Georgie Ripper

ORCHARD BOOKS

www.rainbowmagic.co.uk

Fairies with their pets I see
And yet no pet has chosen me!
So I will get some of my own
To share my perfect frosty home.

This spell I cast. Its aim is clear:
To bring the magic pets straight here.
Pet Keeper Fairies soon will see
Their seven pets living with me!

Contents

Easter Bunny

"Isn't it a lovely day for a party?"
Kirsty Tate said, looking up at the
sapphire-blue sky.

Her best friend, Rachel Walker,
nodded and handed Kirsty a chocolate
egg. Rachel was staying with Kirsty
for the holidays and the girls were
hiding Easter eggs ready for an Easter

party for Jane, Mr and Mrs Dillon's five-year-old daughter.

"There are some great hiding places here," Rachel said, gazing around the beautiful big garden with its green lawns and colourful flowerbeds. She knelt down and hid the egg under a shrub. "Jane and her friends will love the Easter egg hunt!"

"It'll be fun," Kirsty agreed, hiding an egg behind the birdbath.

"How many children are invited to
the party?" Rachel asked.

"Eleven!" Kirsty replied,
her eyes twinkling.
"Mr and Mrs Dillon
are very pleased that
we've come to help
out! They've been
friends with
my mum and dad
for ages, and Jane
is sweet." Then she
lowered her voice.
"Do you think
we'll find another
of the missing pets
today, Rachel?"

"I hope so," Rachel whispered back.
"Let's keep our eyes open!"

Rachel and Kirsty had a special secret: they were best friends with the fairies! Whenever there was trouble in Fairyland, the girls were always happy to help, and trouble usually meant that the mean Jack Frost and his goblin servants were up to no good.

This time Jack Frost had been angry that he didn't have a pet of his own, so he had kidnapped the seven magical animals belonging to the Pet Keeper Fairies. He had whisked them away to his ice castle, but the mischievous pets had escaped into the human world. So Jack Frost had sent his goblin servants to capture them and bring them back.

The Fairy Queen had explained to Rachel and Kirsty that, without their magic pets, the Pet Keeper Fairies couldn't help pets in the human world who were lost or in trouble. So the girls were determined to find the fairy pets before Jack Frost's goblins did.

"Well, we've made a good start," Kirsty pointed out. "Katie the Kitten Fairy was delighted when we returned her magic kitten, Shimmer."

Just then, a pretty little girl with long blonde curls waved to the friends from the back door. "Hello, Kirsty! Hello, Rachel!" she called. She had been upstairs changing into her pink party dress when the girls arrived. Now she rushed towards them, her face alight with excitement.

"All my friends are coming to the party, Kirsty! We're going to have an Easter egg hunt, and then Mummy and Daddy are giving me a special Easter present!" she said excitedly.

"Aren't you lucky, Jane?" Kirsty smiled, as Mr and Mrs Dillon followed their daughter into the garden.

"Jane, come and help me get the presents ready for your guests," said Mrs Dillon, noticing that Rachel and Kirsty were still holding chocolate eggs to hide. "I think Rachel and Kirsty are busy!"

She and Jane went back inside, and Mr Dillon turned to the girls. "It's kind of you to help out," he said gratefully. "There's so much to do." Then he smiled at them. "Would you like to see Jane's Easter present?" he asked.

The girls nodded and Mr Dillon led them to the garage. Inside, sitting on the workbench, was a pet box made of cardboard.

Rachel and Kirsty peeped inside and saw
a fluffy black rabbit with floppy ears,
nestled cosily on
a bed of straw.

"Oh, he's
gorgeous!" Rachel
gasped.

"Jane will love
him," Kirsty added.

Mr Dillon smiled.
"Yes, she will," he agreed.
"She's been pestering us for a rabbit!"

Rachel turned to Kirsty. "We'd
better finish hiding the eggs," she said.
"The guests will arrive soon!"

Quickly the girls hid the remaining eggs
behind flowerpots, trees and the garden shed.
Just as Kirsty placed the last egg behind
a clump of daffodils, the front doorbell rang.

"Here they come!" Rachel said with a grin.

Fifteen minutes later, all the guests had arrived. Soon Jane was dashing around the garden with her friends, looking for the chocolate eggs.

"I've found one!" Jane shouted, her face glowing with excitement.

"Well done!" laughed Kirsty. She and Rachel were standing on the patio, watching. There were shrieks of delight as some of the other children found eggs too.

"OH!" A little girl in a yellow dress suddenly gasped loudly. "Come and see!"

Rachel and Kirsty hurried over to the little girl, who was now kneeling down in front of a tree, peering at the trunk.

"I just saw the Easter bunny!" she announced breathlessly.

Rachel and Kirsty stared at her, puzzled. They hadn't hidden a rabbit anywhere!

"Where?" asked Rachel.

The little girl pointed at a hole in the trunk of the tree. "It came out of there, but now it's popped back in again," she said.

"How do you know it was the Easter Bunny?" Kirsty asked.

"Because it was pink!" the little girl replied.

Rachel and Kirsty glanced at each other in surprise. Then Rachel stared more closely at the hole in the tree, and suddenly, her heart began to race. In front of the hole, she was sure she could see the faintest sparkle of fairy magic!

Vanishing Act

Rachel nudged Kirsty who had just sent the little girl off to look for more eggs. "Look!" she whispered.

Kirsty stared at the shimmering, magical haze in front of the hole and her eyes lit up. "Fairy magic!" she gasped. "Rachel, do you think—"

But before Kirsty could finish, there

was another shout from the bottom of
the garden.

"I've seen the Easter bunny too!"
A little boy was pointing at a large,
leafy shrub and beaming with delight.

Kirsty and Rachel dashed over. They
could hardly believe their eyes when
they saw
a beautiful, fluffy,
lilac-coloured
rabbit, sitting
under the shrub.
But as Kirsty
bent to move the
leaves away, the
rabbit vanished in
a glittering cloud
of lilac sparkles.

"This is definitely

fairy magic!" Kirsty whispered. "The bunny must be one of the fairy pets!"

"Yes, Bella the Bunny Fairy's rabbit!" Rachel agreed.

By now all the children had come to see the Easter bunny.

"Where's the bunny gone?" asked one little girl, looking disappointed.

"I don't know," Kirsty replied quickly. "Why don't you go and look for more eggs?"

"Let's look for the Easter bunny instead!" Jane suggested, and all the children cheered. They began racing round the garden, calling, "Bunny! Where are you?"

"We must find the rabbit and give it back to Bella," said Kirsty. "Luckily, I can't see any goblins around! I wonder where the bunny is now."

Suddenly Rachel's eyes widened and she grabbed her friend's arm. "Look at the picnic table!" she gasped.

Mr and Mrs Dillon had set the party food out on the table while the children searched for eggs. As the girls stared,

they could see a swirl of golden
sparkles hovering over it.

The girls hurried to the table.
Sitting beside a large plate of salad,
nibbling on a carrot, was the magic
bunny, now a sunshine-yellow colour!

Before Kirsty and Rachel could do
anything, Jane spotted the rabbit too.

"The Easter bunny!" she shouted, and
the children rushed over to the table.

"Be careful," Rachel said anxiously, worried that the bunny might disappear again if it got scared.

But Jane gently stroked the rabbit's fluffy head, and it seemed quite happy to be petted. "Isn't it lovely?" Jane sighed. "I wish I had my own bunny!"

"We'd better get the rabbit away before Mr and Mrs Dillon come out," Kirsty whispered to Rachel. "I don't know how we'll explain a yellow bunny! We'll take it to my house."

Rachel nodded. "The bunny's very tired," she announced, picking it up gently. "It's going home now, so say goodbye."

"Goodbye, Easter bunny!" the children chorused, waving. Then they dashed off to search for more Easter eggs.

"I'll tell the Dillons we have to pop home for something," Kirsty murmured to Rachel, running inside.

When she came out again, the two girls carried the bunny around the house and out through the side gate, which they closed carefully behind them. "How are we going to keep the rabbit safe until Bella the Bunny Fairy gets here?" asked Rachel, as they walked along an overgrown path beside the house. "She can't be far away," Kirsty replied. "But maybe we could use the fairy dust in our magic lockets to take the bunny back to Fairyland ourselves."

Before Rachel could reply, the girls heard a nasty sniggering sound above their heads. Alarmed, they looked up to see four green goblins sitting on the branch of a large oak tree, grinning at them.

"Oh, no!" Rachel gasped.

"Let's get out of here!" Kirsty whispered to her.

The two girls hurried on along the path. But, all of a sudden, the ground beneath their feet seemed to disappear.

"Help!" Kirsty cried, as she tumbled into a large hole.

Rachel was too shocked to cry out, but luckily she managed to keep hold of the magic rabbit as she fell. The two girls landed on a bed of soft leaves, and stared at each other in horror.

"The goblins must have dug this hole and covered it with branches!" Kirsty gasped. "They set a trap!"

"And we walked right into it!" Rachel groaned.

"Ha ha ha!" The goblins cackled with glee.

"We were trying to catch the magic bunny, but we've caught two pesky girls as well!" one goblin cried. "Hurrah!"

Bella Breezes In

As Rachel and Kirsty climbed to their feet, the goblins bent over the hole. Before the girls could stop them, one of the goblins snatched the magic rabbit out of Rachel's hands. The bunny squeaked in dismay.

"Give that bunny back!" Rachel shouted crossly, trying to clamber out of the hole.

"Come and get it!" jeered the goblins.

And off they raced round the side
of the house towards the
front garden, giggling
and cheering.

"We mustn't let them
get away!" Kirsty said
urgently, trying to
heave herself out of
the hole too. But it
was just a little too
deep for the girls
to climb out.

"Hang on, I'm
coming, girls!"
called a silvery voice.

Rachel and Kirsty
looked up to see a tiny fairy
surfing through the air towards
them on a large green oak leaf, her

long tawny hair streaming out
behind her in the breeze.
"It's Bella the Bunny Fairy!"
Kirsty said happily.
Bella came to a halt
above Rachel and
Kirsty's heads and
waved at them. She
wore a beautiful,
green halterneck
dress, with a beaded
sunflower at the
waist and neck,
and gold shoes.
"We're so glad
to see you, Bella,"
Rachel said gratefully.
"But I'm afraid the goblins
have run off with your bunny."

Bella nodded. "I knew Misty was around here somewhere!" she exclaimed. "Don't worry, those goblins can't have got far, and I'll have you out of there in two twitches of a bunny's nose!" She lifted her wand, and a shower of golden sparkles floated down onto the girls. Rachel and Kirsty held their breath as they shrank to fairy size, and glittering wings appeared on their backs.

"Good idea, Bella!" Rachel laughed as she flew easily out of the hole, with Kirsty beside her.

"What shall we do now?" asked Kirsty, as the three friends hovered in mid-air, wings fluttering. "How are we going to find the goblins?"

Just then a gruff, angry shout echoed round the garden.

"Follow that sound!" Bella cried, swooping through the air towards the front of the house.

Rachel and Kirsty hurried after her, and the three of them peered round the corner of the house, into the front garden.

The goblins were crouched in some bushes underneath an open window. They were arguing fiercely with each other. One of them, the biggest, was holding Misty.

"There's my bunny!" Bella whispered anxiously, pointing at the frightened-looking rabbit. "Girls, we must save her!"

Bunnies Abound!

The goblins hadn't noticed Rachel, Kirsty and Bella staring at them. They were too busy arguing.

"You do it!" one snarled crossly.

"No, you do it!" another replied.

"I'm not climbing up there!" The first goblin said, pointing at the open window. "I might fall and hurt myself!"

"Coward!" jeered the one holding Misty.

"What are they arguing about?" Rachel whispered.

"Look!" Kirsty replied, pointing at the open kitchen window. A large basket of Easter chocolates sat on the windowsill. "You know how greedy goblins are. They want those chocolates!"

Underneath the window was
a wooden trellis with
a rose clambering up it.
One of the goblins
tried to climb up the
trellis, but it swayed
slightly and he
jumped off
nervously.

"What's the
matter with
you?" another
goblin sneered.
"Scaredy cat!"

"Shut up!" the
goblin roared furiously.

"Poor Misty!" Bella said,
staring anxiously at her bunny.
"She's trembling with fright."

"Why can't she just disappear like she did before?" asked Kirsty.

Bella shook her head. "Misty can't disappear if someone's holding her, or if she's nervous," she explained. "We have to think of a way to get her back!"

While Kirsty and Bella were talking, Rachel had been staring at the basket of chocolates. In the middle of it sat a beautiful, blue toy bunny, which looked very like Misty. Slowly an idea swam into Rachel's mind.

Looking excited, she turned to the little fairy. "Bella, I think there might be a way we can get Misty back! Can you make Kirsty and me human-sized again?"

Bella nodded. She waved her wand and in an instant the two girls were back to normal.

"We need to go inside the house," Rachel whispered.

Looking puzzled, Kirsty and Bella followed Rachel back to the side gate. As Rachel opened it, Bella fluttered down and hid in her pocket.

Then the girls walked into the garden where the children were still looking for eggs. Mr and Mrs Dillon were laying plates on the patio table. "Mrs Dillon, is it OK if I borrow the blue bunny from the Easter egg basket?" Rachel asked. Mrs Dillon looked a bit surprised, but she nodded.

Rachel and Kirsty entered the kitchen. Rachel peeped out of the window and saw the goblins still arguing down below. Then she picked up the toy bunny and gave the basket a little tap. Several of the chocolates fell out and tumbled to the ground outside the window.

"That'll keep the goblins busy for a few more minutes!" Rachel said quietly.

Kirsty peeped over the windowsill. The goblins had pounced on the chocolates and were gobbling them up eagerly.

"Time to head back outside now," Rachel whispered, and Kirsty followed her friend out of the house, through the side gate and over to the hole in the path that the goblins had made.

"Kirsty, can you cover the hole with twigs and leaves like the goblins did?" Rachel asked.

Kirsty nodded and began pulling some fallen branches across the hole.

"Bella, we need a long piece of string," said Rachel. "Can you help?"

"Of course!" Bella agreed, zooming out of Rachel's pocket. She waved her wand, and in a shower of sparkles, a long length of golden cord appeared on the path.

Rachel grabbed the string and tied one end of it around the middle of the toy bunny. Kirsty and Bella watched in amazement. They didn't have a clue what Rachel was up to!

"We're all set!" Rachel grinned, as she finished tying the knot. "Now all we need is Misty's help to make my plan work!"

Goblins Give Chase!

"Tell me what Misty has to do,"
Bella said eagerly.

"We need her to escape from
the goblins for a few minutes,"
Rachel explained, waving the toy
bunny in the air. "Then we'll try to
confuse them with this!"

"You mean, we'll make the goblins

think the toy is Misty?" Kirsty said. "But to do that, Misty will need to be—"

"Blue!" Bella laughed. "No problem!" Lifting her wand, she began to write in the air with it. Like a sparkler, the wand left a glittering trail of bright blue letters, the exact same colour as the toy bunny. The letters spelled out:

"Perfect!" Rachel declared, grinning.

"Now Misty knows exactly what colour blue she has to be!" Bella said with a smile. As the words hovered in mid-air, she flicked her wand and sent them floating round the side of the house towards her pet. The girls followed, eager to see what would happen.

"That's mine! Give it back!"

"You've had lots, greedy guts!"

"Who are you calling greedy guts?"

The goblins were still fighting over the chocolates. Rachel and Kirsty peeped

round the side of the house as Bella's
message floated towards Misty. They
saw the little bunny's nose twitch. And
then, very slowly, the sunshine-yellow
of her fluffy coat began to turn exactly
the same shade of blue as the toy
bunny! At the same time, Bella's
magic message disappeared.

Suddenly one of the goblins noticed
the bright blue bunny.
He could hardly
believe his eyes.
"Look!" he yelled,
jumping up and
down in amazement.
"The bunny's gone
blue!" He stared
suspiciously at the
big goblin holding Misty.

"What did you do to it?"

"Nothing!" the big goblin snapped. "It's not my fault!"

"Ha ha!" one of the others laughed smugly. "If Jack Frost wanted a yellow bunny, you're going to be in big trouble!"

As the goblins began arguing about who'd changed the rabbit's colour, Rachel put the toy bunny on the ground. She kept hold of the other end of the string, and turned to Bella.

"Please turn Kirsty and me into fairies again!" she whispered.

As soon as Rachel and Kirsty had their wings back, the girls fluttered up into the air. Kirsty helped Rachel hold the end of the string, as the toy was too heavy for Rachel to carry now that she was fairy-sized.

"We need Misty to lead the goblins over here," Rachel told Bella.

Bella nodded and began to write in the air with her wand again. This time the message said:

FOLLOW ME

Rachel, Kirsty and Bella watched as the message floated round the side of the house towards Misty. The goblins were pushing and shoving each other now. The one holding Misty was so annoyed he was dancing up and down in fury, and the girls could see that he wasn't holding the bunny so tightly anymore.

As soon as Misty saw Bella's message, she began to wriggle and kick. The goblin was taken by surprise and, in a second, Misty had squirmed from his grasp and was racing towards the side of the house.

"You idiot!" the other goblins shouted angrily. "You've let the bunny go! After her!"

As Misty dashed round the side of the house towards Bella, she began to shrink to fairy pet size. Then the tiny blue rabbit scampered up off the ground and lolloped happily through the air towards Bella.

"Well done, Misty!" Bella cried, and Rachel and Kirsty smiled as the fairy gave her pet a big hug. "Now come with me!"

As Bella and Misty whizzed off to hide behind a tree, Rachel turned to Kirsty. "Here come the goblins!" she whispered. "Ready?"

Kirsty nodded.

A few seconds later the goblins hurtled round the side of the house, grumbling and shouting.

"There she is!" shouted the big goblin, pointing at the toy bunny sitting on the path. "Get her!"

"Head towards the hole, Kirsty!" Rachel whispered.

The two girls began to fly, bouncing
the blue bunny on its string along
the ground below them. Rachel had
been worried that the goblins might
spot the string, but they didn't. Their
eyes were fixed on the toy rabbit,
and they charged after it — straight
towards the hole!

A Magical Easter

Rachel and Kirsty flew on, slowing down a little so that the goblins could get closer to the bunny. The girls bounced it carefully onto the covering of twigs and leaves over the hole.

"I'm going to catch it!" one of the goblins yelled triumphantly, reaching out for the bunny.

"No, let me!" shouted another.

"I want to tell Jack Frost that
I caught it!" a third yelled.

All four goblins made a grab for the
bunny together, and fell on top of the
twigs and leaves in an untidy heap.
A second later the covering gave way.
With shrieks of rage, the goblins all

plunged into the hole, pulling the string out of Rachel and Kirsty's hands and taking the toy bunny with them.

The girls beamed at each other in delight.

"Brilliant plan, Rachel!" Kirsty laughed.

They flew down and hovered over the hole as the goblins climbed to their feet.

"Caught in our own trap!" the big goblin groaned.

"It's your fault!" one of the others moaned. "If you hadn't lost the bunny, we wouldn't be here now!"

"At least we've got the bunny back!" another added, picking it up. Then he gave a screech of rage. "This isn't the magic bunny at all! It's a toy!"

Rachel and Kirsty laughed as he threw the toy rabbit out of the hole in disgust.

"It's a good thing
goblins aren't too
clever!" Rachel said,
as she and Kirsty
flew over to join
Misty and Bella
who had popped
out from behind
their tree.

"Thank you, girls!"
Bella laughed, her eyes
sparkling with joy. "Misty's safe,
and it's all thanks to you!"

"We were glad to help," Rachel
replied.

Misty scampered down to Rachel's
shoulder and nuzzled her ear
gratefully. Then the bunny touched
her nose to Kirsty's, in thanks.

Suddenly, the tiny rabbit turned to
Bella and began to twitch her nose
furiously as she talked to her fairy
owner.

"Girls," Bella announced after
a moment, "Misty told me she came
here because there's a bunny nearby
who needs her help. He's lost!"

As Bella was speaking, Kirsty blinked.
She'd just spotted something: a small
black bunny was poking his nose out
of a nearby bush and staring up at her.

"Rachel, look!" she gasped. "I'm sure that's Jane's bunny. He must have escaped from his box!"

Rachel saw the black rabbit and nodded. "But how did he get out?" she wondered.

"Children, time for presents!" Mrs Dillon's voice came from the back garden, followed by cheers from the children.

Kirsty looked worried. "We have to get the bunny back into his box before Jane opens it!" she gasped.

"Bella, can you turn us back into girls again?" Rachel asked urgently.

Bella waved her wand immediately.

As soon as she was back to her normal size, Kirsty tiptoed across the grass towards the black bunny. He stared up at her with big dark eyes, and to Kirsty's relief, let her pick him up.

"Let's go!" Rachel said, grabbing the toy bunny and untying the string.

Kirsty and Rachel hurried to the garage, followed by Bella and Misty.

The girls could see the children crowding round Mr and Mrs Dillon in the garden, but luckily, nobody noticed them.

"Look!" Bella pointed her wand at the pet box. "That's how the bunny escaped!"

Rachel and Kirsty looked closer at the box and saw that a large hole had been chewed in one side. Carefully, Kirsty popped the little rabbit in through the hole. Then Bella waved her wand and a cloud of dazzling sparkles swirled around the box, making it whole again.

"Right, time for Jane's special present!" Mr Dillon announced, heading for the garage.

"Let's get out of here!" Bella whispered.

Quickly they all hurried out of the garage and went back to the side gate so that they could peep into the garden and see Jane get her present.

The little girl looked very excited when she saw the pet box her dad put down on the grass. She pulled the flaps open, and gave a squeal of delight. "A bunny! My very own bunny!"

She reached in, gently picked the

rabbit up and gave
him a big cuddle.
"Look!" Kirsty
nudged Rachel.
"Is that just the
sunshine, or can
you see a magical
sparkle around Jane and her bunny?"

"Definitely a magical sparkle!"
Rachel said firmly.

"I'm going to call him Sooty," Jane
laughed, beaming at her parents.

"Look at Misty!" Kirsty whispered
to Rachel.

Misty looked just as happy as Jane.
She was so thrilled, she was changing
through all the colours of the rainbow,
from red to violet.

"It's time for us to go,"
Bella said, stroking
Misty's fur. "But
thanks for all
your help, girls.
Enjoy the rest
of the party!"

She blew kisses at them and Misty
twitched her nose – one twitch for Rachel
and one for Kirsty. Then Bella waved
her wand and she and Misty disappeared
in a shower of fairy dust.

"Time for the chocolates, children!" Mrs Dillon called.

Quickly Rachel hurried over and popped the toy bunny back into the basket. The children crowded round Mrs Dillon as she handed out the chocolates.

"The perfect end to a brilliant Easter!" Kirsty said happily.

Rachel was smiling as she watched the children. "Yes," she agreed, grinning at Kirsty. "All the bunnies are with their proper owners!"

Win a Rainbow Magic
Sparkly T-Shirt and Goody Bag!

In every book in the Rainbow Magic Pet Keeper Fairies series (books 29–35) there is a hidden picture of a collar with a secret letter in it. Find all seven letters and re-arrange them to make a special Fairyland word, then send it to us. Each month we will put the entries into a draw and select one winner to receive a Rainbow Magic Sparkly T-shirt and Goody Bag!

Send your entry on a postcard to Rainbow Magic Pet Keeper Competition, Orchard Books, 338 Euston Road, London NW1 3BH. Australian readers should write to Hachette Children's Books, Level 17/207 Kent Street, Sydney, NSW 2000.
Don't forget to include your name and address.
Only one entry per child. Final draw: 30th April 2007.